THE SPECKLED PANIC

Andersen Young Readers' Library

Hazel Townson

THE SPECKLED PANIC

Illustrated by David McKee

Andersen Press · London

Text © 1982 by Hazel Townson
Illustrations © 1982 by David McKee

First published in 1982
by Andersen Press Limited,
20 Vauxhall Bridge Road, London SW1V 2SA.
This edition published 2002.

British Library Cataloguing in Publication Data available
ISBN 0 86264 828 9

Phototypeset by Intype, London
Printed and bound in China

Contents

For Kenneth, who never panics

1

A Magic Purchase

One Tuesday, Kip Slater forgot to buy the toothpaste. His mother had given him two pound coins at breakfast time and asked him to fetch a tube on his way home from school.

'Make sure you don't forget, or there'll be trouble! We haven't a squeeze left in the house.'

All day Kip remembered. Then school ended and he was suddenly caught up in a very absorbing game of football. Kip arrived home at five minutes to six without the toothpaste.

Only as he was hanging up his jacket did the pound coins bounce out of his pocket and remind him of his errand. Kip groaned, chasing the money around the hall-stand, where it finally rolled to a halt behind a boot. He picked the money up and sped off again towards the chemist's shop, never guessing that this journey was to mark a turning point in his whole life.

The chemist's shop was closed. Kip ran on towards the supermarket, but could see from half a block away that this was also closed. All the wire baskets had disappeared from the pavement outside and a man with a big bunch of keys was locking the main door. Kip groaned again. Where else could he get toothpaste at this time of day? The launderette and the fish-and-chip shop weren't much use, which left only Belle's Bazaar.

Belle's Bazaar stayed open until seven. It was a small, dim, crowded shop which sold practically everything. Belle herself was as large as the shop was small; as bright, in her colourful, gypsy-like skirts and blouses, as the shop was dim. Her big smile welcomed you, her gossip held you, but her muddle-headedness finally drove you away.

Kip leapt down the two stone steps, past the loudly-pinging doorbell and into the shadowy Bazaar. Surely somewhere, among all these balls of wool and nappy-pins and tins and cardboard boxes, there was one little tube of toothpaste, with fluoride or without?

'Now then, sonny, what can I get you?'

'Toothpaste, please!' Kip sounded desperate.

'I've only the Purple Speckled. Extra special. Very good stuff, so I'm told.'

Kip could hardly believe his luck.

Grabbing the carton that Belle held out, he quickly paid and escaped before she could change her mind. Belle called something after him, but he didn't stop to hear what it was. He was already late for tea and very hungry. Kip ran all the way home.

8

Only as he handed the carton over to his mother in the brightly-lighted kitchen did Kip glimpse the flowing, red script on the front of it.

'VENGER'S PURPLE SPECKLED TRUTH-PASTE' it said. Or seemed to say.

Not toothpaste, but truthpaste!

It couldn't be that really, of course. It must be just a trick of the eyes, coming in from the dusk to the light.

'What sort's this supposed to be?' asked Mrs Slater. 'Purple Speckled? Never heard of it! Whatever will they think of next?'

'Let's see?'

Kip's dad looked up from his evening paper.

'*I* don't know!' he exclaimed with disgust. 'They give you strawberry flavour and green stripes and rum-and-raisin and I don't know what. Why can't we have honest-to-goodness toothpaste with no fancy gimmicks? They don't do you any good, you know, all these jazzy colourings. You may as well try and clean your teeth with a slice of blackberry tart.'

'Yes, Dad,' replied Mrs Slater patiently. 'I expect it was the name that took Kip's fancy. Caught his imagination, didn't it, son?'

Mrs Slater had not named her son Kipling for nothing.

Kip said nothing. He was concentrating on his sausage-pie-and-beans.

10

Mrs Slater, who carefully cleaned her teeth after every meal, but had long since despaired of ever getting Kip or his father to do likewise, bore off the Purple Speckled as soon as the meal was over. She was still in the bathroom, brushing her teeth, when a knock sounded at the front door.

11

Mr Slater tutted, guessing who it was. The door flew open and in walked the Slaters' next-door neighbour, fat, noisy, untidy Mrs Madding.

'Anybody home?' Mrs Madding called in an over-cheerful voice which set Mr Slater groaning. He couldn't stand Mrs Madding, and could only marvel at the patient, long-suffering way in which his wife put up with her.

'Anybody in?' Mrs Madding called again.

Mr Slater would have liked to say, 'No!' but of course he didn't, and Mrs Madding advanced into the hall, waving an empty teacup in the air.

'Just doing a bit of baking,' she explained, poking her head round the kitchen door. 'Ran out of flour, and of course the shops are shut now. Wondered if I could borrow a cupful off you till tomorrow? I'll bring it back in the morning.'

There was a rushing sound upstairs, and before Kip or his dad could reply to Mrs Madding, Kip's mother appeared on the staircase, flourishing her toothbrush.

'Oh, no you won't fetch it back!' she cried angrily. 'You never do! We're sick and tired of lending you things. What about my egg-whisk, and Mr Slater's screw-driver, and that two pounds of sugar, and the light-bulbs and washing-powder and turpentine and our best deck-chair? We'll never see any of those again. Never! So this time you can jolly-well go and borrow

your flour from somebody else!'

Well!

What a way to talk to a next-door neighbour!

What rudeness, what an unspeakable mouthful of truth!

'Here, Elsie, steady on!' muttered Mr Slater awkwardly, advancing from the kitchen.

Mrs Slater was just as horrified as Mrs Madding. For a few dramatic seconds the two women stood staring at each other, Kip's mother with a hand over her offending mouth and Mrs Madding with the cup clenched to her bosom in shock.

Mrs Slater wanted to call out, 'Oh, dear! I'm sorry!' but she found she could not. Her voice seemed to have frozen in her throat and the only sound that emerged was a croak like cracking ice.

For once in her life, Mrs Madding was utterly at a loss for words. She turned and went, slamming the door behind her. A vase on the hall table wobbled alarmingly.

Now there would be trouble! Now there'd be a street feud worse than the Wars of the Roses! Mrs Slater already dreaded the scenes she knew would follow, yet at the same time she felt glad, relieved, even light-hearted because something had been said that needed saying. Mrs Madding *was* a nuisance, always borrowing things and not returning them. Perhaps now she would stop doing it.

'Hey, Mum, that was great!' cried Kip at last.

'I don't know what came over me!' breathed Mrs Slater faintly. 'I must have gone mad!'

'Come to your senses, more like,' grinned Mr Slater. 'It's not like you to speak out, love, but you only told the truth after all.'

The truth!

Kip had a thought. 'Mum, did you just clean your teeth with that new toothpaste?'

'Yes, I did,' admitted Mrs Slater ruefully. 'And now I ought to go and wash my mouth out with soap and water. That's what I'd tell you to do if you were so rude.'

Kip suddenly bounded up the staircase, heading for the bathroom. He grabbed the toothpaste carton and studied the writing. Just as he had thought! It did say, 'VENGER'S PURPLE SPECKLED TRUTH-PASTE', and the small print underneath read: 'Guaranteed to make you tell the truth for twenty-four hours after use.'

Glory be! What a find! What marvellous, incredible stuff! This was too good to waste on the family. This was a product to be cherished, to have serious fun with at school.

Thrusting the Purple Speckled into his pocket, Kip bolted downstairs again and grabbed his jacket.

'Just going round to Herbie's for a bit!'

'Well, don't forget about your homework!' Kip's dad called after him.

'Not likely!' lied Kip, running off. Just wait until that genius, Herbie Coswell, wrapped his mind round this!

2
Trial Run

Herbie Coswell's young sister Ethel had just swallowed a button. Her mother was thumping her furiously on the back when Kip arrived, and Ethel's frantic struggles were alarming.

Herbie, arms folded, stood watching thoughtfully.

'Turn her upside down,' he suggested at last.

Obediently, Mrs Coswell grabbed Ethel round the waist and swung the child's legs into the air. The button shot out of Ethel's mouth into a dish of green jelly.

'Gosh!' cried Kip admiringly. It was typical of Herbie to stand back calmly and suggest the perfect, the only possible, solution. For Herbie Coswell was a genius. His brain usually reached the finishing-post whilst everybody else's brains were under starter's orders.

Ethel began to yell. The noise was terrible.

'Oh, come on!' said Herbie in disgust. 'We'll go upstairs for some peace and quiet.'

He and Kip marched off to Herbie's bedroom.

'Kids!' Herbie flopped wearily on to the bed. 'Kids

under six shouldn't be allowed to live with us older folks. There should be special colonies, or something.'

'Cheer up!' Kip produced the Purple Speckled. 'I've something to show you.'

'Toothpaste? You gone mad, or something?' Herbie took the package and glanced at the writing on it. Then he sat up and glanced again.

'You've been down to the joke shop!'

'No, I haven't! It's real!'

'Makes you tell the truth? Go on, you've been had! Only torturers and psychiatrists can make you tell the truth.'

'It worked on my mum.' Kip began the tale of Mrs Madding's visit.

'That doesn't prove anything,' scoffed Herbie. 'Your mum was just in a rotten mood.'

'No, she wasn't. My mum doesn't have rotten moods. At least, not all of a sudden, like that.'

'She got fed up with old Madding at last, and no wonder. It was a coincidence that she did it then, when she'd just cleaned her teeth.'

Kip looked crestfallen.

'Mind you,' said Herbie, reconsidering, 'I once read a book about this truth drug that they sprayed over your mouth with a watering-can . . . .'

At that moment, Mrs Coswell called upstairs: 'Herbert! Just you come down here this minute!'

Now, Kip and Herbie knew that if Mrs Coswell called her son Herbert there was trouble in the offing. The boys looked at each other warily, whilst down below young Ethel went on yelling.

'What've you done now?'

'Nothing! I've been good as gold for the last half-hour.'

'Herbert, I'm waiting!' Mrs Coswell sounded like a headsman with his axe at the ready.

Herbie dragged Kip after him to face his mother in the hall.

'Herbert Coswell, you made our Ethel put that button in her mouth. You told her it was a toffee, didn't you?'

'I never!' Herbie was outraged.

'It was a wicked, irresponsible thing to do, and when your dad gets to know. . . .'

'Cross my heart, Mum, I'd never do a thing like that. She might have choked for real.'

'Well, Ethel says you did.'

Herbie turned pink. 'Yeah, she would say that. She loves getting me into trouble, and you always believe her, don't you?'

'I can recognise the truth when I hear it!'

It was the mention of truth that gave Herbie his second inspiration of the evening. He signalled to Kip, who had already read Herbie's mind.

Grabbing Ethel by the hand, Kip dragged her to the bathroom whilst Herbie and his mum continued their argument.

'See the nice purple speckles,' coaxed Kip, squeezing some of the paste on to Ethel's Noddy brush. But Ethel was not in a co-operative mood. She had no intention of cleaning her teeth.

Kip fished in the depths of his pocket and found a plastic canoe from a cornflake packet.

'Brush your teeth and you can have this.'

'Don't want it!'

Kip fished in his pocket again, wondering why Herbie hadn't stuffed a whole boxful of buttons into Ethel's sulky mouth. He came up with a green elastic band, but Ethel didn't want that, either. All that was left, apart from bits of chewed string and bubble-gum, was his grubby handkerchief. He dragged out that disgusting object and regarded it with reverence.

'See that hanky? That used to belong to the Emperor of Japan, that did. He lent it to my grandad, then told him he could keep it. I can't give it you because it's a family heirloom, but you can look at it.'

Ethel stopped crying. She decided she wanted the Japanese Emperor's hanky more than anything else in the world, and made a grab for it. Kip stepped deftly aside. Ethel grabbed again, and at last the deal was made. Obediently, if messily, Ethel began to brush her teeth.

A few minutes later, Kip was able to give the thumbs-up sign to Herbie, whereupon Herbie persuaded his mum to ask Ethel again whether he had made her eat the button.

'No,' replied Ethel meekly. 'Herbie told me not to put the button in my mouth in case I swallowed it.'

Well, after that, young Ethel was sent supperless to bed, and Herbie's mum made a pile of beef-and-pickle sandwiches and a jug of lemonade for the boys to bear

off triumphantly to Herbie's room.

'Now do you believe me? Does it make you tell the truth, or doesn't it?'

'Well, I must admit that wasn't a bad performance. But now you've proved your point, we're not going to waste this stuff on family squabbles.'

''Course not! Why do you think I pinched it from home?'

'We must think,' said Herbie solemnly, 'how best to use this amazing product for the benefit of mankind.'

For a quarter of an hour they did sit and think, the silence broken only by the crunch of pickles and the slurp of lemonade. Then Herbie the genius cried: 'Politicians! Be a nice change if *they* told the truth! We'll start with our own local M.P., and work our way up to the Prime Minister.'

'Super!'

There was a pause, then Kip added: 'How will we get them to clean their teeth with this stuff, though? It was hard enough persuading your Ethel.'

'There are ways and means,' said Herbie, annoyed at being criticised.

'We can't go up to M.P.s in the street and ask them to start brushing their teeth.'

''Course not. We'll get the paste on to their teeth another way.'

'Such as?'

'We'll put it in a cake! It would go nicely in a plain sponge, with a dollop of jam to take the taste away. Blackberry jam, to cover up the purple speckles.'

'Herbie, you're a genius!' Kip told his friend admiringly. But of course Herbie Coswell knew that already.

3

The Wrong Victim

In a few days it would be Speech Day at school, and this year the prizes were to be presented by the local Member of Parliament, Cedric Clodd, an old boy of the school. Cedric did not appear often in his constituency, so when he did, no time was left to waste. He fitted in as many engagements as possible. On the evening of Speech Day, he was also to address the public in St. Bede's Church Hall, to answer any questions the voters might care to put to him.

'That's when he's going to tell the truth,' cried Herbie, 'if we die in the attempt.'

Kip and Herbie knew that after the great, long, boring Speech Day ceremony there would be light refreshments for the Guest of Honour, served in the Headmaster's study. This would be a great opportunity for the boys to slip in the Truthpaste cake among the other goodies. Then they would go to the evening's political meeting and watch the fun.

'Oh, boy!' cried Kip. 'I can hardly wait. My mum's going to ask old Clodd all sorts of questions. She wants to know why the price of school dinners has gone up again, and who put the bus stop in front of my gran's garden gate.'

The two boys carefully laid their plans. If they had spent half as much time on their homework, they would have had Oxford scholarships by the tender age of twelve.

First they bought the sponge cake, which Herbie sliced lop-sidedly across the middle with his penknife. Then they spread the bottom piece with jam sneaked from Mrs Slater's larder. Next, they squeezed some of the Truthpaste over the jam, flattening it down with a lolly-stick. When the cake was ready they put it in an old shortbread tin in which Herbie had once kept caterpillars. Then they took the tin to school and hid it in Herbie's desk.

'How can we be sure old Clodd will eat some of the cake?' Kip wondered.

'Cedric Clodd won't refuse a wedge of cream cake,' replied Herbie with confidence. 'You know how fat he is. My dad says he's just plain greedy. Anyway, after that boring afternoon he'll be ravenous. He'll probably scoff three pieces at least.'

'It's a good job the Head never touches cake. Him and his blooming crispbread and raw carrots!'

The next problem was how to get the cake into the Headmaster's study at the proper time. This was where Fate took a hand. On the morning of Speech Day their

form-master asked for two volunteers to help carry the tea things from the kitchen to the Headmaster's study. Kip and Herbie managed to get themselves chosen for this enviable task, but even then their troubles were not over. Their every move was watched with dark suspicion by Mrs Emmett, the Domestic Science teacher, who accompanied them back and forth along the corridors with tray-loads of crockery, dainty sand-wiches, biscuits and jam tarts. The look in Mrs Emmett's eye proclaimed that she had counted every crumb and teaspoon and would know at once if one went missing.

It was lucky for the boys that Mrs Emmett was also in charge of first aid. Somebody had a fall in the gymnasium and Mrs Emmett was suddenly called away.

'Fine time to have an accident!' she tutted, not happy at leaving two hungry, growing boys with all that food. But of course she had to go.

'Quick! Now's our chance!'

Herbie raced for the tin. Kip rapidly divided the cake into eight, and was just dusting away the crumbs when in walked the Headmaster himself, George Dykes, M.A.

Mr Dykes was in a good mood. He enjoyed Speech Day. He loved showing off in his best suit, and he enjoyed the tea-party in his study afterwards. It had become something of an occasion.

As he walked into his study now, carrying a begonia plant for the party table, Mr Dykes was positively sparkling with happy excitement.

'My word, that's a fine spread!' he exclaimed. 'You've done a good job there, Slater and Coswell! In fact, I think you've earned a small reward. Here, try

some of this!'

Mr Dykes picked up the plate of Truthpaste cake and handed it to Herbie.

Herbie was shocked. 'Oh – er – thank you, sir, but it's nearly dinner-time.' He managed a sickly grin. 'Stew today, sir. Don't want to lose my appetite.'

'Your self-control does you credit, Coswell, but I've never known a boy yet who couldn't make room for an extra piece of cake. Go on, now, take one.'

Groaning inwardly, Herbie was forced to obey.

'Now you, Slater.'

'N-no thank you, sir, really. There might not be enough to go round this afternoon.'

'Nonsense, boy, there's enough food here to feed a rugby team.'

'But – it will spoil the look of the cake if there are two pieces missing.'

'I never heard such rubbish!' cried Mr Dykes jovially. 'Anybody would think you'd just stuffed that cake with poison! Hurry up, now, or the bell will go.'

Kip, too, was compelled to accept the Headmaster's well-meaning offer.

'Well, go on, eat it! I suppose you're shy at standing there eating in front of me, is that it? All right then, I'll have a piece with you. I don't usually eat cake, but just this once. It certainly looks delicious.'

Herbie, having taken the first careful bite, avoiding the Truthpaste filling, nearly choked.

'I wouldn't if I were you, sir. It's a bit peculiar, actually.'

'Peculiar? Then I must certainly try it before I offer it to my guest. Can't give peculiar cake to our Member of Parliament, eh? Might bring the government down!'

The Headmaster took a massive bite from his piece of cake and Kip almost groaned aloud.

'H'm!' remarked the Headmaster, chewing heartily.

'It's certainly different! Very nice. Sticks to your teeth a bit, that's all.' In two more expert bites Mr Dykes finished his portion and sucked a stray blob of jam from his finger.

'Come on, boys! Eat up! Time you were off back to your classes.'

Herbie had stuffed a lump of cake into the top of each sock and was now busily chewing nothingness. As for Kip, he had sidled towards the wastepaper basket and managed to drop his cake into it unnoticed.

'You know, Slater,' Mr Dykes said suddenly, 'I've always wondered why your parents called you Kipling. Such a strange first name for a boy. Your family's not related to the author, I suppose?'

'Oh, no sir! My mum just fancied it, I think.'

'How thoughtless! The other boys must tease you unmercifully. Might have ruined your whole school career for you, a name like that.'

'Oh, I don't mind, sir. It could have been worse. She could have picked on Mowgli.'

'Really!' Mr Dykes sounded quite exasperated. 'I do think parents ought to consider this matter of names more carefully. It was selfish, foolish and short-sighted to say the least . . . .'

The Headmaster's telephone began to ring, and the two boys thankfully made their escape.

'Phew! We're really in trouble now!' gasped Herbie.

31

'All that about your name was the hidden truth coming out, like it did with your mum and Mrs Madding. Goodness only knows what he'll say on the platform this afternoon.'

'No need to worry about that. He writes his speech out and keeps looking at his notes.'

'Suppose what he's written is just polite lies? He won't be able to say it. Anything could happen!'

'You mean – he might say rude things about Cedric Clodd, or the governors or somebody? Oh, he wouldn't dare!'

'He just said rude things about your mother.'

'Yeah, I suppose he did.'

Herbie looked thoughtful. 'Perhaps we ought to kidnap him or something. Hide him somewhere until the truth wears off.'

4

The Chase

Anyone who has ever tried to kidnap a Headmaster will know that it is not an easy matter. Although Kip and Herbie racked their brains all through the rest of morning lessons, they got nowhere. The best thing they could think of was an urgent telephone call which would remove Mr Dykes from the scene. But what sort of call? Had he a mother who might be ill? A sister who might suddenly elope with a penniless actor? They could not tell, for Mr Dykes was a bachelor whose family background remained a secret. That left business. Could he be summoned to a Headmasters' Conference in Brighton? Or to see the Minister of Education? Or to meet a school inspector arriving from London? All these suggestions, the boys decided, lacked the ring of truth. Mr Dykes would immediately check.

'What then?' Kip asked wearily as the dinner-bell sounded.

'We could own up. He might let the Deputy Head take over.'

'Own up – and risk getting expelled or something?

Not likely!'

'Well then, we can find a cure. That's the only chance left.'

'A CURE?'

'You said you bought that stuff at Belle's Bazaar. Maybe she can help us. We'll go now. We've only about two and a half hours before Speech Day assembly, so we'll have to move fast.'

'But what about our dinner?'

'Miss it, of course. There are more important things than food.'

Kip was not sure he agreed with this, but he had not time to argue, as Herbie was already dragging him away. The boys managed to slip out of school unnoticed. They crossed the playing-fields, dived through a hole in the fence and ran all the way into town.

Madame Belle had her coat on, and was turning round the card on the glass door to read CLOSED instead of OPEN. It was her lunch-time, too.

'Don't go!' yelled Herbie, banging on the glass.

Belle hesitated, then decided to open the door.

'Be quick, then!' She let them into the shop. 'Not eating today, boys? Saved your dinner money to buy something more lasting, maybe? Penknife, compass, stamp album ... ?'

The boys dived straight into their Truthpaste story.

'Oh, that!' Belle remembered the carton. 'It was a

sample I had from a traveller. Not meant for sale really. I was going to try it out myself, but you were in such a state that night, I gave it you.'

Kip groaned. 'Which traveller left it?'

'Well, I don't really know, dear. He was new, you see. Ever such a nice little red-head, but he hadn't been here before. Still, he must have left a card. Let's see if we can find it.'

Belle took from a drawer a bundle of little cards printed with salesmen's names and addresses. Agonisingly slowly, she sorted through them until at last she came up with a green one.

'Here it is!'

Both boys craned forward and were able to read, in bold, black lettering:

A. VENGER. CURES, COSMETICS, CLEANING PRODUCTS.

TELEPHONE 4988.

'Venger's Purple Speckled!' cried Kip. 'It's the same name! He must make the stuff himself. We've got to find him.'

'Come on, we'll ring him up.'

There was a telephone box round the corner, but no reply from the number on the card. Kip began hunting through the Vs in the directory to find an address.

'Venables, Venet, Venetian Blinds Ltd., Venner, Venning . . . not a Venger in sight.'

'He must be ex-directory.'

'That settles it. We'll just have to go back and own up.'

'Suppose so.'

Gloomily, the boys began to move away in the direction of school. Then suddenly, Herbie gripped Kip's arm.

'There he is, across the road! Little red-head with a suitcase showing initials A.V.!'

'Talk about luck!'

The two boys rushed across the road, risking death or maiming as they wove recklessly through the traffic. Pedestrians gasped and motorists honked their horns.

'Hey, wait!'

'Mr Venger! Just a minute!'

But the little red-head had not heard them. He walked fast along the pavement, head down, shoulders slightly hunched, eyes on the ground. He was deep in thought. Before the boys could catch him up, Mr Venger reached a bright red mini, and took a bunch of keys from his pocket.

'Stop! Wait for us!'

It was too late. The mini drew away from the pavement as they reached it.

'Huh! Some luck that turned out to be!'

'It's okay. Venger's a traveller making calls. He'll stop again soon. All we have to do is catch him up.'

They flew along the High Street in the direction the red mini had taken. Cargrove's factory was emptying for the lunch-hour and there seemed to be millions of people on the pavements, most of them intent on bumping into Kip and Herbie. Hot, bruised and breathless, they battled on for quite a distance, then Herbie, glancing up a side-street, saw the mini again, parked outside a house.

'Told you!' cried Herbie triumphantly.

'Car's empty.'

'Can't be far away. Let's look in the car for clues.'

They crossed to the mini and pressed their noses against the glass. Kip could see a tartan rug. Was that a clue? Maybe Venger was bound for Scotland. Herbie spotted a half-eaten bag of caramels.

'He might have gone to the dentist's.'

Suddenly Kip felt a hand on his shoulder.

'Now then, what's going on here, eh?' Kip looked up into the face of a policeman.

'This your dad's car, then?' asked the policeman, keeping a tight grip on Kip and reaching out for Herbie, too.

'Er – no, we were just – just looking.'

'Looking for what?'

'Clues. We wondered where the driver had gone.'

'Tried the door, did you?'

'No!' Herbie was indignant.

'Well, that's how it looked to me. Very serious offence, breaking into parked cars. Could get you into a lot of trouble.'

'Honest, we were only looking.'

'Anyway, shouldn't you be at school? I thought you young 'uns from St. Bede's weren't allowed out in the dinner-hour.'

'We're doing a special errand.'

'Yes, something for Speech Day.'

'Speech Day today, is it? Then you'd better get back to school quick. Come on!'

In the iron grip of the policeman, Kip and Herbie were obliged to start walking away from the mini.

'Like a lift back to school?'

The policeman indicated his own car, parked across the road.

'Oh, no thanks!' Kip could just imagine the Headmaster's face if they rolled up to school in a police car after being out of bounds.

'We can walk there in five minutes.'

'Well, see that you do! Straight down this High Street and no turning back. I shall be watching you all the way.'

Releasing his grip at last, the policeman gave the boys a couple of gentle pushes to start them on their way. Kip and Herbie began walking.

Neither boy dared turn round. Maybe the policeman was following them. On and on they walked. Only when the police car drove past them at last did they stop, watch it disappear, then turn and double back towards the red mini.

The car had gone.

'Of all the rotten luck!'

'That's *your* fault, overdoing things as usual,' grumbled Herbie.

'I like that! Whose idea was it to peer into the car in the first place?'

'Well, all right then, you come up with a better idea.'

'I will! Let's have some lunch,' replied Kip, indicating the Snowball Snack Bar a couple of doors away.

'Lunch? Is that all you can think about?'

'Well, we aren't going to catch old Venger. We may as well go back to school and own up, and I'd do that a lot better with a snack inside me. We've missed our

school dinner now.'

Reluctantly, Herbie realised how hungry he was.

'I suppose a quick sandwich wouldn't do any harm.'

They wandered into the snack bar. Kip handed some money to Herbie.

'Get me one egg-and-cress and a rock bun. I'll find us some seats.'

The snack bar was crowded with mid-day customers, and a pall of cigarette smoke hung gloomily round the yellow plastic lampshades. Kip made his way to a far corner and flopped into the only empty chair he could see. All that excitement had sapped his strength. He ate a couple of sugar-lumps for immediate sustenance, then noticed someone leaving. He leapt up to grab the chair for Herbie. Only as he dragged it back to the table did he notice that the person at the very next table, eating hungrily away behind a propped-up newspaper, was none other than A. Venger himself.

5

Mischief with the Mustard

Herbie came struggling along with a tray. Before he reached the table, Kip started pulling faces. Herbie failed to get the message, and Kip actually had to take hold of Herbie's ear and swivel the lad's head in the right direction before the penny dropped.

'Glory be!' Herbie could hardly believe his eyes.

'Well, go on, you're nearest! Ask him for the cure!'

Herbie plonked down the tray. 'Suppose he won't tell us? It's his secret, after all. You wouldn't go blabbing your secrets to all and sundry, would you?'

'You mean, he could stuff us up with any old tale?'

Herbie bit confidently into his sandwich. 'Not if we catch him in his own trap. Get the Truthpaste out.'

Herbie then leaned across to Mr Venger's table and asked if he might borrow the mustard. The little red-head looked up from his newspaper. Two very bright blue eyes stared curiously at Herbie. Then Mr Venger handed over the mustard before turning back to his newspaper and his soup.

'Right!' hissed Herbie. 'Squeeze some Truthpaste into that mustard, quick!'

When he had finished his soup, Mr Venger exchanged the bowl for a plate of sausage-and-chips already waiting at his elbow, and began to tuck in again, still reading his newspaper.

Kip stirred the mustard vigorously with its little spoon, so that the purple Truthpaste speckles were hidden and the stuff took on a more mustard-coloured hue. Then he handed the pot to Herbie, who in turn reached over and passed it back to Mr Venger.

'Thanks! Best mustard I ever tasted!'

There was an anxious moment while Mr Venger continued eating. Perhaps he didn't like mustard. What a pity if they'd wasted all that Truthpaste! But the boys need not have worried, for Mr Venger began to spoon out quite large dollops of mustard, which he flicked on top of his sausages. Then he spread the mustard evenly with the tip of his knife, cut off a piece of sausage and ate it.

'Now for it!' breathed Herbie excitedly. He had actually leaned an arm on Venger's table, ready to pose the all-important question, when the coughing fit began.

Mr Venger flailed helplessly about in the grip of a sudden and terrible cough. His cheeks grew red, his eyes streamed, he groped wildly at the edge of the cloth and pulled it half off the table. Crockery slid to the floor.

Diners turned round in concern. Someone thumped Venger smartly on the back, and someone else tried to offer him a glass of water. Kip and Herbie were appalled. What had they done? The Truthpaste hadn't had this effect on anybody else. Perhaps it was just a bit of sausage gone down the wrong way, but even that made them feel guilty.

Retribution was at hand, in the shape of a plump, cross waitress who bore down upon the boys, shouting angrily: 'Hey, you two! I saw you, messing about with the gentleman's mustard-pot. What you up to, eh?'

'We were only . . .' Kip began, but the waitress had no intention of listening to excuses.

'Out!' she cried mightily, heaving Kip to his feet and Herbie after him. Before they knew it, the boys were at the door of the snack bar, clutching their rock-buns and protesting in vain. The waitress opened the door and pushed them through it.

'Kids ain't supposed to come in here without an adult, anyway!'

As she spoke, a dark blue figure loomed up in front of the boys. It was the policeman who had moved them on from the red mini.

'Well, well! Looks like I shall have to give you that lift back to school after all. Forgotten the way, have you?'

6

The Truth about Truth

The boys were saved by Mr Venger himself, who dashed out of the snack bar, eyes still streaming, cheeks still red.

'Just a minute, Officer!' croaked the red-head, waving his handkerchief. He was only just in time. Kip was already on the back seat of the police car with Herbie being bundled in beside him. The policeman turned, and Mr Venger began to explain that he wanted to talk to the boys.

'It could be a matter of life and death.'

'Oh?' Now the policeman was really interested, but Mr Venger hastened to say that he needn't concern himself.

'Just a private matter.'

'All the same, these lads aren't supposed to be out of school.'

'You're absolutely right, Officer. I'm just going to take them back there. No need for you to trouble.'

Thankfully, Herbie backed nimbly out of the car.

'Now then!' began Mr Venger sternly when the boys were seated in his own car. 'You've a lot of explaining to do.'

Mr Venger knew his own Truthpaste when he tasted it. What he could not understand was how these two boys had got hold of it. It seemed he had a crisis on his hands.

Arthur Venger, it must be pointed out, was no mere salesman, but a genuine artist, a man of original ideas, the actual creator of the goods he sold. In fact, Arthur thought of himself as a crusader. He had once looked up the word 'crusade' in the dictionary and it had said, 'an enterprise against some public evil'. Now, as far as Arthur could see, there were so many public evils that he scarcely knew where to begin. Litter was one, and he was at present engaged upon a cure for litter-dropping. Telling lies was another, and his Truthpaste had been, at one stage, his favourite invention. He remembered vividly the day when that particular recipe had turned out right at last. He had brushed his teeth with the Truthpaste and tried to say, 'Another failure!' only to find that he could not. All that emerged from his throat was a croak like cracking ice. For 'Another failure!' would have been a lie. The experiment had succeeded.

Yet success was not so simple. This was one experiment which Arthur soon wished he had never started.

'Well? I'm waiting to hear your story.'

Herbie nudged Kip and Kip began the tale.

As he listened, Arthur Venger could scarcely believe his ears.

'Are you saying that tube of Truthpaste was on sale in a shop? But it can't have been! I decided to destroy it all. Except for one sample tube, that is. I always keep one of everything I make, just for reference.'

'Destroy it all?' Herbie was horrified. 'But it's great stuff! Can't you sell it? Surely it's worth a fortune.'

Arthur Venger shook his head sadly.

'Truth's a terrible thing, as I soon discovered.'

He had made the stuff, he said, in all good faith. He had worked hard on his recipe, thinking only of what a better world it would be when lies disappeared for ever. Yet when he had tried out the stuff, he had soon found there was more to the business of truth than he had thought.

'That Truthpaste turned out to be downright dangerous. So I altered my recipe to make ordinary toothpaste instead.'

'Dangerous?' Kip echoed fearfully.

'Yes, indeed! I'll tell you a few home truths about truth. You can tell it and nobody believes you, which is enough to drive you frantic. Or you can try hard not to tell it in case you hurt somebody's feelings. Or you can think you're telling it when you're not. Or you can tell it with the best intentions and cause a whole lot of trouble. That's only the beginning. Just you think

about it for a while and you'll end up with a list of complications as long as a cold, wet Sunday.'

'You mean to say it's all right to go around telling lies, then?'

'No, no; I mean there are moments when it's not wise to tell the blunt, straightforward truth. You could break somebody's heart, or make an enemy for life, or even start a war.'

'He's right, Herbie! Look at all the trouble that Truthpaste has caused since we got hold of it. First my

51

mum's outburst, then your Ethel getting sent to bed, then Mr Dykes eating that cake when he wasn't supposed to . . . .'

Mr Venger began to look alarmed. 'Who's Mr Dykes? *He* hasn't tried any Truthpaste, has he?'

'Well, as a matter of fact . . . .'

Arthur began to groan as the story continued.

'Why, the man might say anything! And Speech Day on top of it all! A public audience and newspaper reporters! We must do something right away!'

'Now you're talking!' said Herbie.

'How much time have we got?'

'Oh, Speech Day's a long, boring business. Before Mr Dykes gets going there's the orchestra and the school song and that. Then the Chair of the Governors drones on for ages, and the choir does its madrigals and stuff. We've a good bit of time yet.'

'We'll need it!' said Arthur grimly, letting in the clutch and roaring noisily away.

7

One Green Bottle

Arthur Venger lived outside the town, in a remote little bungalow, littered with ingredients, samples and dirty pots and pans. It was just as well that Arthur lived alone.

When he and the boys reached the house, Arthur rushed at once into the kitchen and unlocked the door of a cupboard marked 'EXPERIMENTAL ONLY'. Inside there were four shelves filled with bottles, jars and packages of various shapes and sizes. Arthur began to shuffle these about with growing anxiety, searching for one particular package. It was not there. Something else was there, though, which should not have been: an ordinary tube of toothpaste made from Arthur's own recipe, no longer at the EXPERIMENTAL ONLY stage. There had been a mix-up!

The little salesman took out a ledger in which he entered his shop visits. He ran his finger down a column of names and stopped at Belle's Bazaar.

'You're right! I left it there by mistake. How careless! I'm as good as a criminal, I am!'

For a moment, Arthur stood horrified. Then he

pulled himself together.

'No use moaning. What we have to do is make a cure. You'll have to help me, or we'll never finish in time. Do as I say, and be very careful. Check everything twice over, to make sure you've got it right.'

As he spoke, Arthur Venger began to fill a huge pan with water, which he set on the stove to boil.

'Here are the scales. Weigh 50 grams of this blue stuff and 25 grams of the green.'

Delighted to be helping, the boys obeyed.

'And when you've done that, chop these leaves up as fine as you can, then scatter them on the boiling water.'

The little kitchen began to fill with steam and peculiar odours. It took them well over an hour to produce a bottle of dark green liquid which Arthur held up to the light and studied intently. He shook the bottle, watching the colour cloud over. He sniffed it thoughtfully. Then he poured a few drops into the bottom of a glass, dipped his finger into the glass, then touched that finger to the tip of his tongue.

'H'm!' He frowned and kept silent for a minute, then his tone suddenly changed.

'Right, that'll do! I'll just lock you two boys in the cellar, then drive off to school with this cure for your Mr Dykes.'

'You'll WHAT?'

'Lock us in the cellar? But we helped you make

the cure.'

'Yes, and you caused all the trouble in the first place.'

'But to lock us up and leave us! You wouldn't do that!'

'Oh, yes I would!' Arthur grinned nastily. 'I'd enjoy it!'

The boys were astounded. This was a turn of events they had not expected. Was Arthur Venger a madman after all? They should never have accepted a lift from a stranger. Here they were, in a remote place where nobody would hear their cries for help. It was time to panic.

Then, as suddenly as it had changed before, Arthur Venger's mood changed again. He began to laugh merrily.

'It's all right. I was just trying out a few lies. I had to see if this stuff worked, and it does. We've done it!'

Herbie noticed the clock. 'But it's already half-past two. We're nearly too late.'

They made a hasty departure, leaving the house in a wild, untidy mess. They jumped into the car, and now Arthur, needing to drive, had to hand over the bottle of dark green liquid to Kip, who was sitting in the front seat.

'Just you be careful with that. A lot of people's futures depend on it, especially ours.'

56

They drove at a fast pace, back into town and out at the other side. Kip was sure they were speeding, and hoped they would not be spotted by their policeman.

The little red mini, followed by a yellow baker's van, had just turned into the lane that led up to school when the accident happened. There was a car coming fast down the middle of the lane towards them. Mr Venger pulled sharply over to the side to keep out of the way, then realised there was still not enough room. He pulled up in a screaming swerve, and the yellow van behind ran into the back of him.

The noise of the impact was much greater than the damage, but even so, Herbie was thrown forward from the back seat, so that his head butted Kip in the shoulder. Kip's arm jerked under his seat-belt, his door flew open and the green bottle shot from his grasp into the roadway, where it shattered and ran green into the gutter.

There was a stunned and terrible silence. Venger and the boys stared at the ruin of their plans.

Then the driver of the baker's van began shouting, and the tableau came to life. Arthur climbed out to inspect the damage and to exchange notes with the others. A little crowd of spectators began to gather.

Kip stared into the hedgerow, envious of the lucky dandelions, while Herbie tried to imagine what his mother would say when he told her he had been expelled from school.

The boys might have gone on sitting there, feeling sorry for themselves, if they had not heard the sound of an approaching police-car siren. In fresh panic, they scrambled from the car and started off at the double on the last half-mile to school.

8

The Purple-speckled Speech

The school orchestra had played its screeching best, the Chair of the Governors had sat down, the last late parent had scurried to his seat, and Mr George Dykes, M.A., had risen to address the Speech Day audience.

There was a respectful hush.

'I must say I am surprised,' Mr Dykes began, ignoring the sheaf of notes on the table beside him, 'to see so many of you here today. The pupils, of course, are here because they have no option, but as for you parents, I can't think why you bother. You must find the whole thing very boring.'

There were one or two shy giggles from the audience, who didn't quite know whether this was supposed to be a joke.

'However, now that you are here,' Mr Dykes went on, 'I suppose you will expect to hear me deliver my report upon the last school year. I'd much rather not. It wasn't a good year at all. In fact, I think the best word to describe it would be DISASTROUS. We didn't win a single cup. Our football first eleven lost all but two of its games, our cricket team averaged seven runs a

match, our girls' hockey eleven injured two referees and we couldn't even find a good enough competitor for the Inter-Schools' Chess Tournament.'

Some of the audience began to look interested. This was certainly an unusual approach to the year's achievements.

'At the last athletics meeting,' Mr Dykes went on, 'our runners came last in the hundred and two-hundred metres, our relay team was disqualified for cheating and our javelin thrower killed a sheep.

'On the academic side, perhaps we did a little better. We produced a language set which invented its own French dialect, and one star handwriting expert who managed to get his name in the Guinness Book of Records – on every page.'

By now a movement could be detected in the audience, a seething restlessness, as people turned to see what the general reaction was.

'You will be wondering what all this means,' continued Mr Dykes, warming to his subject. 'It means, quite simply, that this is not an exceptional school, alive with exceptional geniuses, but a draughty, shabby building where imperfect human beings make mistakes and fail examinations and let down their friends and feel ashamed, and wish they'd never heard of Saint Bede.'

'Hear, hear!' said a tiny voice at the back of the hall.

This produced a ripple of uneasy laughter and a

creaking of chairs and a shuffling of feet. The reporter from the *Grumpton Argus* was seen to be scribbling furiously, and Mr Bigley, the Deputy Head, frowned fiercely round the hall to try to restore some sort of order.

Mr Dykes took a sip from his glass of water before proceeding.

'I could stand here telling you tales about boys and girls who have moved on from this school to Higher Education. Believe it or not, we do have a few. I usually spend half an hour boasting about their successes. But today I'm not going to. Today I'm going to give the true picture of everyday life in this school by describing instead a random sample of achievements.'

Mr Dykes glared around, as if daring anyone to stop him.

'In Form 9E, for instance, we have one boy who has broken no less than seventeen windows during his stay with us, yet still does not know the meaning of the word "fragile". In the same form, another boy has carved twenty-nine messages on our furniture, yet still cannot spell "united".'

By now the hall was holding its breath. There was a sense of alertness such as had never before been felt in a Speech Day gathering. Not one eye was closed, not one surreptitious comic was being read. Some people were actually beginning to enjoy themselves. Not Mr Bigley, though, and certainly not the Chair of the Governors, who thought Mr Dykes had gone mad.

'We have one girl,' Mr Dykes was now saying, 'who has dyed her hair no less than five different colours in the space of one term. If that is not an achievement, I don't know what is.'

This time there were not even any giggles. Nobody wanted to make a sound, for that might cause them to miss the next sensation.

'In Form 8C we have a lad who has uprooted more young trees than any single vandal of his age in the whole of England, while in Form 9E the total number of days lost through truancy last year was nine hundred and four.'

That did it! Mr Bigley swung round in his seat and whispered to the woodwork master behind him, 'This has gone far enough! We must get him off the platform.'

'How?' the woodwork master whispered back.

'Take him a message, or something. Use your ingenuity, man!'

'Who, me?'

This was the moment at which Kip and Herbie tiptoed into the hall, having run all the way from the accident in the lane. They had not tiptoed far before they saw their worst fears were realised. Mr Dykes really had started telling the truth.

'Each year I talk about the parents' role in education,' he was saying now. 'A most important role. This year I'd like to begin at the beginning with the naming of the child. One boy in this school has been given, for instance, an author's surname for his own first name. Now, I want you to think . . . .'

Inspired by the sheer horror of the situation, Kip shot forward and grabbed Mr Bigley by the arm.

'Sir!' shouted Kip. 'There's a dangerous explosive device in the hall. I think you ought to clear the building.'

9

An Explosive Afternoon

Normally, Mr Bigley would have quelled such a disturbance with one cold and terrifying look. Today, however, he felt only that his prayers had been answered.

At once he leapt on to the platform and requested an orderly evacuation of the building. The explosive device would probably turn out to be harmless, he said, but of course they could take no chances. The Speech Day ceremony was postponed until further notice.

People began at once to scramble to their feet. Teachers barked orders and classes started to file out of the hall at a much brisker pace than usual. Most parents looked flustered, but they soon got the hang of things and began following their offspring to the exits. It was a wonderful display of discipline and self-control, a well-rehearsed performance which the *Grumpton Argus* would be obliged to admire.

Mr Bigley then had time to turn his attention to the Headmaster. Where was he? And how quickly could he be spirited away before he said anything more? Mr Dykes had led his platform party in a brisk but dignified withdrawal to the far side of the front lawn, and was there discovered guarding the school's new mini-computer which had only just been paid for.

'Are you all right, Headmaster?'

'Of course I'm all right, Bigley. What the dickens is going on?'

'Everything is under control,' answered Mr Bigley evasively, 'but I think you had better come along to the sports pavilion where you'll be safe. I'll round up the other VIPs to join you there. Perhaps Mrs Emmett could lay on some tea.'

'Tea?' echoed the irate Headmaster. 'It's police we need, not tea. Let me know the minute they arrive. I'll talk to them.'

'But, Headmaster, I think you should . . . .'

'Don't stand there chattering, Bigley! This is an emergency!'

It was obvious that poor Mr Bigley's efforts to spirit the Head away were useless. He could only hope that in the confusion nobody would remember what Mr Dykes had said, or take notice of anything else he might say from now on.

Meantime, reporters from the *Grumpton Argus* and the *County News* were bombarding Cedric Clodd with questions. Did Cedric feel that the present emergency had been aimed at him? Was this bomb a wicked attempt by his political opponents to prevent him from making his speech?

Cedric would have loved to say yes. He longed to feel important enough for an assassination attempt. Unfortunately, he had arrived late owing to a rail strike, had had no time for lunch, and had therefore been given a quick cup of tea and a slice of Truthpaste cake just before he went on to the platform. When he opened his mouth to agree with the reporters, he suddenly found that he could not. All that emerged from his throat was a croak like cracking ice. Most embarrassing!

Luckily for Cedric, the reporters' attention was diverted by a bandaged Arthur Venger, who now rushed upon the scene, crying loudly:

'It's all my fault!'

Naturally, the reporters thought Arthur was about to confess to planting the bomb, and they turned eagerly towards him, pencils poised.

'Truthpaste, that's the trouble!' cried Arthur, seeing chaos and and fearing the worst. He plunged feverishly into his story, wanting only to make a clean breast of the whole thing.

It was an amazing story. It was the sort of story that newspaper reporters dream about, whilst they are writing up vicarage garden fêtes and local weddings and amateur operatic performances. It was, in fact, a scoop, which could have made not only the local headlines, but the national and international ones as well. The only snag was that the two reporters did not believe it. Faced with the pure, unvarnished truth, they could do no more than throw long-suffering glances at one another behind Arthur Venger's back, and quietly conclude that the man was crackers.

Meanwhile, someone had dialled 999, and soon the screech of sirens heralded the arrival of police and ambulance. Kip and Herbie, waylaid by Mr Bigley, were dragged forth to tell their story – to the very same policeman who had haunted them all day.

The policeman groaned. 'I don't believe it!'

'Anything wrong, Constable?'

'It's these kids, Sarge. Known offenders. Ten to one you'll find they're at the bottom of everything.'

'All right, leave 'em to me. You go and locate the explosive device and get the details down.'

The sergeant turned to Kip and Herbie with a suspiciously friendly smile.

'Now then, lads, let's hear from you. WHAT explosive device are we talking about exactly?'

Kip looked hunted. He licked his lips carefully before replying: 'It was Mr Dykes, sir. He could have brought the house down at any minute. We felt he was a human explosive device.'

10
The Final Truth

That evening, St. Bede's Church Hall was packed for Cedric Clodd's address. Word had gone round of the afternoon's excitement, and people thought Cedric really had been the cause of the trouble. So everyone was here to see what further thrills might happen.

As for Cedric himself, he had been deprived of his afternoon glory and was determined to make up for it tonight. This would be the best speech he had ever made. His words would ring with high ideals and loyalty and self-sacrifice, and at the end he would be given a standing ovation.

'Ladies and gentlemen, constituents, friends,' he began. 'The true purpose of my being here to-night . . . .'

There followed a sort of croaking sound, then a long, alarming pause. Had Cedric, perhaps, been poisoned? There was a stir of interest. Then the words that Cedric had planned to say mysteriously changed themselves into very different words.

'The true purpose of my being here tonight is to show off. I love showing off. Best of all, I enjoy the sound of my own voice. (You must admit I have perfect elocution and my words carry clearly to the farthest corners of the hall.) I don't really care about your problems, although now and again I pretend to, so that you won't forget to vote for me next time. I also need to do a bit of work for you now and then in order to get my name into the newspapers. (That's something I *do* enjoy, as long as they spell it properly.) But really, you know, this is a very boring job, especially the journeys I have to make up here. What a dump this town is! I can't think how you can stand living here!'

There were shouts of shock and protest from the audience.

'How dare he talk to us like that?'

'Well, at least he's honest,' one voter yelled above the rest. 'That's more than you can say for most.'

'Oh yes, I'm honest all right!' retorted Cedric, surprising even himself. 'I'm so honest that I'll tell you all, here and now, that I'm no good to you. I possess none of the qualities of a useful Member of Parliament. In fact, now I come to think of it, the best advice I can give you is not to vote for me at the next election after all. Not even if I'm the only candidate.'

'Can't say fairer than that!' cried somebody in the front row.

'No, by Jove, I've never heard such straight talk from a politician.'

72

'Here's a chap we can actually believe at last.'

'True as steel, he is!'

'Genuine as Harris tweed!'

'He's another George Washington, bless his spotless soul!'

There was no doubt that the crowd was impressed. The comments grew warmer and more generous, until somebody burst into song. In no time at all the crowd was singing with gusto:

'For he's a jolly good fellow

And so say all of us!'

At the back of the hall, Kip, Herbie and Arthur Venger looked astoundedly at one another. Arthur began to steer the boys towards the door.

'Come on, this is no place for us! May as well go and get on with that litter-dropping cure. See if that will be less of a disaster than the Truthpaste has turned out to be.'

'Oh, I don't know,' replied Herbie the genius thoughtfully. 'It may not be such a disaster as you think. Suppose we sold it to the enemy . . . ?'

But that's another story.

About the Author

Hazel Townson was born in Lancashire and brought up in the lovely Pendle Valley. An Arts graduate and Chartered Librarian, she began her writing career with *Punch* while still a student. Reviewing some children's books for *Punch* inspired her to write one herself. Fifty-four of her books have so far been published and she has written scripts for television. *The Secrets of Celia* won a 'best children's book' prize in Italy and *Trouble Doubled* was shortlisted for a prize in the North of England. She also chairs the selection panel of the Lancashire Children's Book of the Year Award. Hazel is a regular visitor to schools, libraries and colleges and her books have been described as 'fast-moving and funny'. She is widowed with one son, one daughter and four grandchildren.

The One-Day Millionaires
Hazel Townson
Illustrated by David McKee

Arthur Venger, inventor of the notorious
'Truthpaste', has a brilliant new scheme to
make everyone feel more generous. But when
villains cash in on his idea to make a fortune
for themselves, chaos ensues.

'A funny and fast-paced story for fluent readers'
Independent on Sunday

ISBN 0 86264 835 1
£3.99 paperback (U.K. only)

Coughdrop Calamity
Hazel Townson
Illustrated by David McKee

Inventor Arthur Venger and his two young
helpers produce a cure for the common cold,
but they have reckoned without the
unscrupulous Bruno Kopman who will go to
any lengths to preserve his Comical Cough Sweet
business – (a joke on every wrapper). Also hot
on the trail is Doctor Yess who wants the cure to
sell to his rich Harley Street patients. Theft,
kidnapping, corny jokes and mayhem lead to a
devastating conclusion.

ISBN 0 86264 834 3
£3.99 paperback (U.K. only)

Trouble on the Train
A Lenny and Jake Adventure
Hazel Townson
Illustrated by Philippe Dupasquier

On a train trip to a Manchester museum, Lenny
overhears a sinister-sounding conversation. Has
he stumbled across a plot to blow up the train?
He tries to pass on a warning, but nobody will
believe him. So he and Jake take matters into
their own hands, ending up in a life-
threatening situation from which they have to
be rescued by a *girl*!

This is the fifteenth story in Hazel Townson's
popular *Lenny and Jake* series. The last story,
The Clue of the Missing Cuff-link, was praised by
the *Independent on Sunday* as a 'fast, funny and
hugely entertaining read'.

ISBN 0 86264 624 3
paperback

TROUBLE DOUBLED
including
Dads at the Double and Double Snatch
Hazel Townson

Two exciting mysteries by Hazel Townson are combined in this paperback original.

Dads at the Double
After meeting at a Schools Drama Festival, Paul and Sara, who live at opposite ends of the country, begin a correspondence. But their letters gradually uncover a horrifying truth which could devastate the lives of both families.

Double Snatch
Angela's weekend visits to her estranged detective dad involve her not only in his caseload but also in a frightening drama which puts her best friend's life at risk.

'The action is artfully advanced through correspondence'
Daily Telegraph

ISBN 0 86264 710 X
£3.99 paperback (U.K. only)